Echoes in Time

By Victoria Capps

Chapter 1: The Invitation

Growing up, they always asked the same questions: *How will you change the world? What will you leave behind? Can you save humanity?*

 Most people let those questions fade as they get older. For me, they became a shadow that never left. A reminder that we know better but rarely do better. Some try. Some fight. But the truth? It's never enough. During my time with the Program, I've witnessed things no one on the outside would believe—miracles, fractures, ripples through reality itself. Outsiders call it the *Mandela Effect.* They say we misremember. That our minds play tricks. But I know better. I've watched history shift beneath my feet, entire events rewritten as if they never happened. The greatest blessing—and the greatest curse—is knowing that the ripples are real. We are making a difference. But the cost is heavy, and the Program is still only in its early trials.

Today is different. Today, they're bringing in new recruits.

I've heard the rumors. Some are pulled in through desperation—addicts bought out with the promise of a clean slate in exchange for loyalty. Others are drawn from the underground, shadow networks with their own secrets, kept separate from the rest of us. And then there are the idealists: the ones who want to reverse wrongs, repair the timeline, maybe even heal the Earth itself. They're the ones who dream of erasing centuries of hatred. Of restoring what was stolen.

I've only ever been stationed here, at this facility, but I know there are others scattered across the world. Sometimes I imagine what it would be like to see them, to step outside of this place. To see the bigger picture.

This morning, they sent us into the fields. A sea of flowers and trees stretched for miles, the air crisp like an apple freshly picked. The sunlight poured down in a soft yellow glow, the breeze wrapping me in warmth like nature itself was holding me close. Calm. Perfect. Eternal.

Only it wasn't.

It was a simulation—a glimpse of what the world *could* be. Calm, beautiful, untouched. A reminder of everything we've already lost.

If I've lost you, let me take a step back.

I hadn't even heard of the Program before I was recruited. At the time, I was chasing mysteries—fascinated by why people think the way they do, why they act as they act. I was obsessed with the *why*. Why criminals feel no guilt. Why violence and power get passed down like an inheritance. Why politics erase instead of protecting. And, more than anything, why humanity keeps repeating the same mistakes.

I wanted to save the world. Didn't we all? Some people stop caring. Others run straight into the fire, creating ripples that crash like tsunamis. I was one of them. Marches, protests, rallies—I was there. Fighting for human rights, for Black lives, for LGBTQ+ lives. Faces blurred into crowds, but sometimes strangers stood out, watching too closely. Then people began disappearing. Rumors of trafficking rings. Thousands missing, children swallowed by a system that was supposed to protect them. Bodies turned into empty shells.

Even through the chaos, I never imagined it was connected to something bigger. That the disappearances, the lies, the history rewritten—it was all part of the same fracture. Maybe the world has always been this terrifying. Maybe the only difference is that now, fear is mainstream. Fear is how they control us.

Police who sow chaos just to step in as saviors. Laws that strip freedoms, all in the name of safety. A system that keeps us obedient because we're too afraid of what happens if we disobey.

And in the middle of it all, the Mandela Effect. At first, I thought it was just memory games—movie quotes that never existed, brand logos changing overnight. But then I remembered an ad from the nineties: a celebrity going door to door handing out checks. Clear as day. Yet when I searched for it, nothing. No record. The celebrity himself swore it never happened. I wasn't alone. Thousands remembered the same thing. How do you explain that? Mass delusion—or rewritten reality? That was when the Program found me.

It was at a rally, loud and raw, our voices filling the streets. A leader I'd never met pulled me aside. His words were simple, but they carried weight: *"If you want to change the future, you have to start with the past."*

I didn't understand then. Not fully. But I do now.

Since joining, my job has been to recruit, the same way they recruited me. Most people think I disappeared into a private college somewhere, chasing an education. If only they knew the truth—that I wasn't just studying. I was learning how to bend time. How to shift memory. How to fight for a future we've been denied.

They say it's complicated. But really, it's the simplest thing in the world.

We all want someone to be proud of us. To look at what we've given back to others and to the world and say: *you mattered.*

That's all I want. And maybe—just maybe—that's why I was chosen.

Chapter 2: The History Lesson

The first thing I learned here is that history is never history—it's edited memory.

Today, that lesson hit harder than ever.

Our new class was supposed to be about "truth and perspective," though the schedule just called it *History Module 2*. The door opened, and in walked Professor Smith. Tall. Stern. A face like stone. The kind of man who looked like he'd never smiled in his life.

Then he opened his mouth.

"Fact or Myth." He scrawled the words across the board in looping chalk strokes, and just like that, the ice cracked. His voice carried a strange energy, sharp but playful, as though he was daring us to keep up.

"Mila," he said suddenly, his eyes pinning me in place. "Give me one."

Caught off guard, I blurted out the first thing that popped into my head: "Atlantis."

The class snickered, and I wanted to sink into the floor.

"Great," Smith replied without hesitation. "Now, which side do you put it on—fact or myth?"

I hesitated. "...Myth?"

"Good. Next."

The names rolled down the roster—Jalen, Kimberly, Kyle—until the board was crammed edge to edge with events. Lost civilizations. Civil rights movements. Alien sightings. Ancient massacres. Some names I knew. Others I had never even heard of.

Then Professor Smith leaned against the desk, scanning the list. "Do we agree? Or should anything move?"

The room shifted with nervous energy. No one wanted to be wrong. Then Kimberly spoke.

"I think Columbus discovering America should be moved to myth."

All eyes turned. She pressed forward. "He didn't discover anything. The land was already inhabited. He brought disease, stole resources, and claimed a seat at a table he was never invited to."

Silence. A charged silence. Even Smith froze for a heartbeat, then slowly nodded. "And how many agree?"

Hands rose—hesitant, then firm.

Next was Kyle. "Aliens should be fact. There are too many strange events, too much evidence."

Professor Smith tilted his head. "Evidence?"

Kyle shrugged, his voice steady. "Not proof. But enough to make me wonder."

Smith smiled faintly. "Then prove it. You'll all get a chance to prove it."

He divided us into groups; each assigned an event from the board. Research. Reports. Evidence. Our job wasn't to regurgitate what we'd been taught, but to uncover what was buried. What had been erased.

My group was assigned the Tulsa Race Massacre. Theodora got the Greensboro Four.

The deeper we dug, the heavier it felt.

Tulsa, 1921. A thriving Black community. Doctors, lawyers, teachers. Homes, businesses, prosperity—all burned to the ground by white mobs in a single night. Hundreds were dead. The survivors forced out by new laws that made it impossible to rebuild. A genocide buried under silence.

Reading it, I felt my chest tighten. How many lives, how many generations of brilliance, were erased because of greed and hate? What inventions were never created? What leaders never born?

Theodora's group reported on the Greensboro Four. Four young men who refused to leave a whites-only lunch counter in 1960. They sat. They endured insults, violence, humiliation. And their quiet defiance sparked a movement that spread like wildfire. A ripple that became a wave.

Listening to her, I realized something: the walls in this place aren't just made of concrete and steel. They're made of silence. Silence built by people who wanted history forgotten.

As we regrouped, Smith scanned the room, his eyes bright. "Do you see now? The difference between what you've been taught and what's true? How easily truth is rewritten when those in power control the pen?"

I swallowed hard. Because I did see it. Too clearly. And for the first time, I wondered—if they can erase *that*, what else have they buried?

Chapter 3: The Selection

We were supposed to be heading to our next class when Mrs. Gwen stopped us in the hall. Her sudden appearance was enough to ripple through the group—whispers, rumors, nervous laughter. No one ever pulled students off schedule unless it mattered.

"I heard she faked her death to get here," someone muttered.

"No, I heard she told her family she had a government job so secret she couldn't even say the name," another whispered.

The door creaked open, and Mrs. Gwen stepped inside, bringing the stragglers with her. She waited until the room had gone silent before she spoke.

"Hello. I am Professor Gwen—but you may call me Mrs. Gwen." Her tone was calm but sharp enough to cut the air. "I'm sure you're wondering why you've been chosen. What we discuss here does not leave this room. Not to your friends. Not to your families. Not to anyone. If this information spreads, it could cause panic—or worse, fall into the wrong hands."

Every eye fixed on her.

"You were selected because each of you has knowledge or instincts the Program needs. Some of you excel in history, others in conspiracy research, others in physics and frequencies. Together, you are our next phase. We've been running tests—planting propaganda in present-day timelines, monitoring how the public reacts. But our real work…" She paused, letting the silence stretch. "…is time travel."

The room froze.

"Small jumps so far," she continued. "Within the past ten years. But even those have caused… complications. Operatives stranded. Missions compromised. That's why you're here. With your combined skills and the resources of the Program, we believe we can succeed where others have failed. And perhaps even bring our people home."

Her eyes swept the room, sharp and unyielding. "This is a choice. Accept, and you'll be fast-tracked into advanced training. Decline, and you'll continue in your scheduled classes—valuable, but ordinary. If you step forward, you may never be able to speak of it again. You may never be the same again. But you will have done what no one else on Earth has: traveled through time."

She passed a single sheet of paper across the desks. A confidentiality agreement. At the bottom, in small type, was the warning: *Violation will have consequences.*

I felt my heart hammering as the pen touched my hand. Time travel. Was this what I had been pulled here for all along? Could it even be real? Or had it always been real, hidden from us until now?

One by one, we signed.

When the papers were collected, Mrs. Gwen gave a small, knowing smile. "Good. Then it begins."

We were split into teams and escorted deeper into the facility. I found myself grouped with Theodora in history, which was a relief. Jalen was assigned to theories and conspiracies, and Chris to frequencies and physics.

Mrs. Gwen's parting words echoed in my head as we walked.

"Certain places on Earth vibrate with unusual frequencies. Some are natural. Some are not. We believe they may cause glitches in our systems—faults that distort time itself. Whether coincidence or design, we don't yet know. That's what you will help us uncover."

Time travel. Glitches. Lost operatives.

And for the first time since I arrived, I wasn't just curious.
I was afraid.

Chapter 4: New Assignments

Mr. Winters was waiting for us when we entered the briefing room, a sleek laptop open in front of him. His presence filled the space—calm, but heavy with authority.

"Listen carefully," he said, eyes flicking across the group. "We've lost contact with several operatives. Their last known mission was a time jump into Washington, D.C., June 2022. Since then—silence. We don't know if they failed to return or if they… landed elsewhere."

He tapped a key, and two photographs appeared on the screen.

"Alex. Sarah. Your assignment is to find them—or at least find out what went wrong."

The faces burned into my mind. Alex: slender, glasses, brown skin, sharp eyes. Sarah: pale, curly red hair, a grown-up Shirley Temple. They looked ordinary. They weren't.

"The history team will work with me," Winters continued. "Scour news archives, digital traces, anything that might reveal their movements. Jalen, Chris—you'll assist Dr. Evans with frequency analysis. These jumps depend on matching the energy of a specific moment. If the frequency shifts, the destination can shift too. We need to know if that's what happened here."

Theodora and I dove into the records first. We searched protests, arrests, articles scrubbed from the web. Roe v. Wade had just been overturned then—a decision that ripped through the nation. People flooded the streets. The perfect cover for a mission.

"What if they were there to plant propaganda?" Theodora muttered as she scrolled. "Shift public opinion, sway the moment."

"Or stop someone else from doing it," I added. "Depends on who's pulling the strings."

Hours blurred by. Then—finally—something.

"Got her," I whispered. A mugshot flickered on my screen. Sarah. Arrested in Georgia. Charges: false documents, disorderly conduct.

"Georgia?" Theodora frowned. "That doesn't make sense. Why detour hundreds of miles away?"

We flagged Winters immediately. He leaned in, studying the image. "That's her. But if she was in Georgia, it means the frequency shifted. They missed their return window."

At the same time, Jalen and Chris returned, their faces pale. "We found the anomaly," Jalen said. "The D.C. location measured at thirty megahertz on departure. By the time of their scheduled return, it had dropped to five. That kind of drop could have rerouted them anywhere."

Chris added, "A local band was playing near the protest. Their sound equipment was operating at thirty megahertz. If Sarah tried to jump back, then..."

"She would have locked onto the wrong frequency," Jalen finished. "Georgia."

We all stared at each other, the weight of realization sinking in.

But that wasn't the strangest part.

When I looked at Sarah's mugshot again, something inside me twisted. A memory I wasn't supposed to have. I saw her. Not in Georgia—in D.C. At the protest. I remembered the noise, the chaos, the fight breaking out in the crowd. And her face—watching. Searching.

But I had never been there.

Had I?

The room seemed to tilt, and from the looks on Jalen's and Theodora's faces, I knew I wasn't the only one.

We were remembering things that shouldn't exist. And if Alex and Sarah had been there—maybe they wanted us to.

Chapter 5: Glitches

I thought I had grown used to strange. Time travel. Lost operatives. Alternate histories. Signing a contract that basically said *don't speak*.

But nothing prepared me for the glitches.

It started small. My necklace—one I wore every day— was gone. Not misplaced. Gone. As if it had never existed. Then my matching ring—my mother's gift— changed shape. It was now part of a set I didn't remember owning, though she swore she'd given it to me years ago.

Next, my files. Notes I'd saved during our search for Alex and Sarah scrambled into gibberish. News articles twisted into versions that had never happened.

I told myself it was exhaustion. Stress. Too many late nights. Until Jalen slipped.

We were in lab, buried in data, when he looked up and said, "Rebecca—hand me that file."

I froze.

"What did you just call me?"

He blinked, confused. "Didn't I say Mila? Weird—I swear I saw your name change on the screen for a second."

I laughed it off, but my stomach knotted.

Later, the dorm wing gave us our proof. Posters we had hung weeks ago had... shifted. Not their design, but their message. One that had once read: *No justice, no peace* now screamed: *Order keeps us safe.*

I pulled up the photo I'd taken when we first hung it. Same image. Same poster. Different words.

It wasn't just me.

Theodora burst in, pale. "The court case I found earlier? The one we pulled for Sarah? It's gone. Not hidden. Not redacted. Just... never existed."

Chris scanned the files, his voice low. "It's like the data's fighting itself. One version overwriting another every few minutes—two realities stacked on top of each other."

Dr. Evans joined us, his expression grim. He listened, silent, then finally spoke.

"These aren't Mandela effects. They're temporal echoes. The timeline isn't stable anymore. You're remembering two versions of reality at once—because both technically exist."

The air in the room seemed to thin.

"How is that possible?" I asked.

Evans hesitated. "Someone—or something—is sending ripples through time. A jump went wrong. Or worse—an unauthorized one was made."

The words settled over us like ice.

Chris's voice cracked. "You think it's Alex?"

Evans didn't answer right away. When he did, his voice was heavy.

"I think we're standing at the start of a fracture. A split timeline. And if it widens…"

He didn't need to finish. We all felt it—the walls of reality beginning to bend.

Chapter 6: Echoes of the Past

I've stopped trusting my own memories.

Not because they're wrong—because they're right when they shouldn't be.

Today, I remembered something that never happened. At least, not in this version of reality.

I was sitting on marble steps. A protest roared in the distance—Roe v. Wade, D.C., 2022. But this wasn't research. It was real.

Alex sat beside me, his face tired, his eyes far older than they should've been.

"You think this program is about fixing the past?" he asked. His voice carried weight, the kind that comes from knowing too much. "It's not. It's about rewriting it, so no one remembers how broken it really was."

I remember asking, "Then why stay?"

His answer cut through me like glass. "Because someone has to leave breadcrumbs for the ones who still think."

And then—nothing. Like someone slammed a door on the memory.

Back in the lab, Theodora looked up from a stack of redacted files. Her voice was hushed. "Mila… do you ever feel like he wanted us to find him?"

I nodded slowly. "Not just find him. Remember him. Remember what they made us forget."

Chris broke our silence, sliding into the chair beside us. He had something pulled up on the monitor—satellite logs, encrypted data normally locked behind top-level clearance. "This shouldn't even exist. But someone accessed it last week. From a public terminal. In Atlanta."

He cracked the encryption. An audio file flickered to life.

And then—Alex's voice.

"If you're hearing this, the timeline has fractured. I don't know which version of you is listening but trust the memories that don't make sense. Those are the real ones. They'll erase this message soon, but you need to move quickly. They're coming for the ones who remember."

The recording cut.

Silence swallowed the room.

Finally, Jalen leaned forward, his jaw tight. "If Alex is sending messages through frequencies, and we know high-vibe zones cause distortion… we could trace him."

Chris nodded. "Like a breadcrumb trail through the noise."

Theodora's eyes locked on mine. "If we do this, we can't go back. Not to safety. Not to ignorance."

My throat was dry, but I forced the words out. "We were never safe. They just made us forget we weren't."

Outside, the wind rattled the windows, carrying a strange metallic undertone—like static before a storm.

I looked up. For a heartbeat, the sky flickered.

A glitch.

The timeline wasn't holding.

And maybe... that was the point.

Chapter 7: Breadcrumbs

Jalen's fingers flew across the keyboard, the glow of his monitor painting his face in shifting blues and greens. "Coordinates trace back to Atlanta," he muttered. "But the signal's fragmented. Like something's… embedded."

Chris leaned over, headphones pressed tight. A low hum filled the lab, a frequency that seemed to crawl beneath the skin. "It's not just static," he said, his voice tense. "There's music under it."

He filtered the noise, and faintly, a melody emerged. A haunting refrain layered with hidden tones.

"You remember what they forgot…

 Turn back the clocks, connect the dots…"

Chris froze. "It's not just a song. It's a code."

We mapped the tones, each note aligning with letters. Slowly, the message formed:

JULY 4TH. MEET AT SITE ZERO. FOLLOW THE STATIC.

Silence pressed down on us, heavy and electric.

"Site Zero?" Jalen whispered.

Theodora pulled up the Program archives, fingers trembling. "According to the earliest files, Site Zero was where the first successful timeline shift took place.

But it was sealed. Off-limits. No one goes in without clearance."

"Then we stop asking permission," I said, my voice firmer than I felt.

We packed quickly, each of us handed a small tuner device Chris had rigged to scan for residual frequencies. "If Alex left more messages, these would find them," he said.

As we left the facility, the hallway lights flickered, buzzing faintly like insects caught in glass. Then the intercom hissed, a whisper bleeding through the static—one word, stretched and broken:

"Remember."

We froze, the hair on the back of my neck rising. Theodora's grip tightened on my arm. "Did you hear—"

"Yes," I whispered.

The timeline wasn't just shifting anymore. It was speaking.

And Alex's trail had only just begun.

Chapter 8: Site Zero

The Fourth of July came too fast.

Fireworks exploded somewhere in the distance as we slipped through the back entrance of the facility. The night sky glowed red, then green, then white, each burst masking our footsteps.

Chris's tuner pulsed with faint static, guiding us like a compass.

"Down," he whispered, pointing to a maintenance stairwell.

The air grew colder as we descended, concrete walls slick with condensation. At the bottom waited a steel door sealed with biometric locks—fingerprint, retina, voice. A dead end for anyone else.

But Alex had thought ahead.

A panel at the base was cracked, wires exposed. Chris crouched, his hands steady as he spliced into the system. The static from the tuner bled into the lock.

The screen flickered.

Then the door groaned open.

The smell hit us first—dust, metal, something chemical. The air tasted stale, like it hadn't been touched in decades.

We stepped inside.

The chamber was massive, carved into stone, humming with faint residual energy. In the center stood a machine—half broken, half alive. A web of coils, copper wiring, and glass tubes, glowing faintly as though clinging to memory.

"This is it," Theodora whispered. "The original jump device."

Jalen circled it slowly, awe mixing with fear. "It's not just tech. It's… alive."

I felt it too—the vibration in my bones, the way the air seemed to shift with every breath. Like the machine remembered.

Then Chris's tuner beeped sharply. He held it up, eyes wide. "Signal spike—someone left a recording."

A hidden projector clicked on, casting grainy footage across the wall.

Alex.

He looked exhausted, thinner than when I'd last seen him in my fractured memory. His eyes darted off-screen before locking onto us.

"If you found this, good. That means you're still listening. Site Zero is where it all began—and where it has to end. The machine doesn't just shift time. It fractures it. Every jump creates another branch, another version of us. They've been hiding it, rewriting what doesn't fit. But the branches don't go away. They echo."

He leaned closer, voice urgent.

"Find the echoes. Follow them. Before they collapse— or before they collapse *us*."

The screen went black.

For a long moment, none of us spoke.

Then the floor beneath us rumbled. The machine whined, coils sparking faintly as if awakened by Alex's words.

Theodora's whisper broke the silence. "It's not dormant."

Chris swallowed hard. "It's waiting."

The rumble deepened, echoing through the chamber until it felt like the walls themselves were breathing.

And for the first time, I understood why they sealed this place.

Site Zero wasn't just a relic.

It was alive.

Chapter 9: The Machine Awakens

The machine hummed louder, a low vibration that rattled the floor beneath our feet. Its coils pulsed with faint blue light, like veins carrying blood.

Chris backed away, clutching the tuner. "That's not residual energy. It's active."

"No one's used this thing in decades," Theodora whispered. "How is it—"

Her words were cut off by a sharp crack. Sparks leapt across the copper wiring, throwing jagged shadows against the stone walls.

Then came the sound.

Not mechanical. Not electrical.

Whispers.

At first, I thought it was the others, but their lips were sealed, their eyes wide. The sound came from the machine itself—layered voices speaking in fragments.

"...July fourth... fracture... remember..."

I staggered back, my pulse racing. "It's talking."

Jalen shook his head; eyes locked on the coils. "Not talking. Echoing. It's bleeding fragments of other timelines."

The whispers grew louder, overlapping until the air felt heavy with words. My vision blurred. For a heartbeat, I wasn't in Site Zero anymore.

I was standing in a classroom—Professor Smith at the board, writing *Fact or Myth.* The next blink, I was on marble steps with Alex again, his voice cutting through the noise: *"Leave breadcrumbs."*

Then—chaos. Fire in the streets. People screaming. My mother calling my name.

"Mila!"

Theodora's voice yanked me back. I gasped, trembling, sweat slick on my palms. The chamber was spinning, the machine roaring.

Chris slammed the tuner against a panel. "I can stabilize the frequency—just give me a second—"

"Don't!" Jalen shouted. "We don't even know what it's tuned to! What if stabilizing locks us into the wrong timeline?"

The machine shrieked, a high-pitched wail that pierced bone. Then, as suddenly as it began, it went silent.

We stood frozen in the aftermath, the only sound our ragged breathing.

On the machine's console, new text had burned itself into the screen. Words that hadn't been there before.

**ECHO ONE INITIATED. TRACE THE
FRACTURE.**

No one spoke.

Because deep down, we all knew what it meant.

We hadn't just activated the machine.

We had started something.

And there was no going back.

Chapter 10: First Echo Mission

We stood in silence around the console, the words still burning across its screen:

ECHO ONE INITIATED. TRACE THE FRACTURE.

Chris adjusted the tuner, its dial spinning wildly until it locked onto a frequency—sharp, piercing, alive. The chamber trembled in response.

"This is it," he whispered. "The first echo."

The machine's coils lit with a blinding pulse. A ring of light expanded outward, shimmering like liquid glass. For a moment, I thought it would swallow us whole.

Theodora grabbed my hand. "Ready or not," she breathed.

And then the floor dropped.

The world bent sideways. My stomach lurched as colors smeared into each other—red, gold, blue, all melting into black. A static roar filled my head, and then—silence.

When I opened my eyes, I was standing in the middle of a city street. But not the one I knew.

The buildings looked familiar, yet wrong storefronts rearranged, logos twisted, traffic lights glowing the wrong colors. A newsstand displayed headlines that made my chest tighten.

TULSA THRIVES: AMERICA'S GREATEST CITY

Theodora read over my shoulder, her voice cracking. "Tulsa... survived."

It wasn't the massacre. It never happened. This Tulsa was alive thriving, pulsing with energy.

People walked past us, elegant in clothes that shimmered with designs I couldn't name. Hovering trams zipped overhead. And yet, beneath the wonder, there was unease. The faces looked... blank. Smiling too perfectly. Movements too synchronized.

Jalen's voice was low. "This isn't just a repaired timeline. It's curated."

Chris checked the tuner. "Frequency stable. We're locked here until we find the fracture."

That word echoed in my head. *Fracture.*

Then I saw it—down the street, a billboard flickering like bad reception. One moment it read *UNITY IS STRENGTH,* the next *OBEDIENCE IS FREEDOM.* Back and forth, back, and forth, as if two realities were fighting for dominance.

"There," I said. "The fracture point."

We moved cautiously, weaving through the crowd. The closer we got, the louder the static in my head became. My vision blurred—two versions of the same street overlapping, colliding. One thriving. One burning.

At the base of the billboard, a smear of graffiti appeared, words scratched in red paint that pulsed as though alive:

REMEMBER WHAT THEY ERASED. —A

My breath caught.

Alex had been here.

Theodora touched the paint, her fingers trembling. "This is his trail. He wants us to see this."

Before I could answer, the ground shook. The billboard crackled, splitting into shards of light. The crowd around us froze, every head turning in unison toward us, their smiles stretching wider, eyes too bright.

"Uh… Mila?" Jalen said, his voice tight. "I think we've been noticed."

The static roared again, drowning everything else.

And then the world fractured.

Chapter 11: The Fracture Fights Back

The crowd turned in unison, their too-perfect smiles stretching wider, eyes glinting with unnatural light. For a heartbeat, no one moved. Then the first man stepped forward. His movements were fluid but wrong—like a puppet tugged by invisible strings.

"Target identified," he said, though his lips didn't quite match the words.

The rest followed. Hundreds of voices speaking in eerie harmony:

"Target identified. Target identified. Target identified."

Jalen swore under his breath. "They're not people. They're echoes."

The static in my skull pulsed like a heartbeat. I stumbled back, but Theodora yanked me forward.

"Run."

We bolted down the street, weaving through frozen storefronts and glitching signs. The echoes followed, their footsteps perfectly synchronized, voices droning louder with every block.

Chris clutched the tuner, its dial spinning wildly. "The signal's destabilizing! If we don't anchor soon, we'll be stuck here!"

"How do we anchor?" I shouted over the static roar.

He didn't answer—he was too busy adjusting the tuner, sweat dripping down his temple.

Theodora grabbed my arm and pointed. Ahead, the billboard still flickered between two realities—*UNITY IS STRENGTH / OBEDIENCE IS FREEDOM.*

"The fracture's there!" she yelled. "We break it, we anchor!"

We skidded to a stop at its base. The graffiti glowed brighter now, Alex's words pulsing with light:

REMEMBER WHAT THEY ERASED.

Jalen slammed his palm against it. "This is his anchor! This is how he wants us to stabilize!"

The echoes were closing in, their chanting voices now a single deafening roar:

"Target identified. Target identified."

Chris twisted the tuner's dial, locking onto the graffiti's frequency. A beam of sound shot out, harmonizing with the billboard's flicker.

And then everything exploded.

Light fractured around us, shards of reality colliding like broken glass. For an instant, I saw two versions of Tulsa overlaid—the thriving utopia and the burning ruins. The air crackled with the weight of both truths.

Theodora screamed, "It's collapsing!"

"Hold the frequency!" Chris yelled back.

I pressed my hand to the graffiti, the words burning hot beneath my skin. And then, just for a second, Alex's voice whispered in my ear.

"You're close. Follow the echoes."

The light surged—then snapped.

The crowd vanished. The billboard froze, solid, locked into one version. The city fell silent.

We collapsed onto the pavement, gasping. Theodora was shaking, her eyes wide. "What the hell was that?"

Jalen's voice was grim. "Proof. The fractures aren't just alternate timelines. They're defenses. Someone doesn't want us finding the truth."

Chris stared down at the tuner, its screen now glowing with new text.

ECHO TWO: ACTIVE. TRACE THE NEXT FRACTURE.

We had survived the first Echo.

But the machine wasn't finished with us.

Chapter 12: Echo Two

We didn't return to Site Zero the way we left it.

One moment we were gasping on Tulsa's pavement, the next darkness. A suffocating silence broken only by the hum of the machine.

The console flickered:

ECHO TWO: ACTIVE. TRACE THE FRACTURE.

Theodora's voice trembled. "We don't even get a choice this time."

Chris steadied his tuner. "Hold on."

The chamber bent. Light dissolved. And then we were gone.

When the world reformed, we were sitting at a lunch counter.

The stools squeaked under our weight. The air smelled of stale coffee and grease. A faded *WHITES ONLY* sign hung above the counter, the letters flickering in and out like faulty neon.

I knew this place. So did Theodora. Her face had gone pale. "Greensboro," she whispered. "1960."

The static crawled in my ears. A second later, the room shimmered. The sign vanished, replaced by one that read *UNITY DINER – OPEN TO ALL.* The walls brightened, repainted in cheerful colors. Happy families filled the booths.

Two versions. One layered over the other.

And at the center of it all sat four young men at the counter. The Greensboro Four. But they were wrong. Their faces blurred, shifting between real and artificial, their voices looping in broken phrases.

"…we will not… we will not… we will not move…"

"…progress is peace… peace is obedience…"

It was like the protest itself had been split—one version fighting for freedom, the other twisted into propaganda.

Jalen's jaw clenched. "They're using the sit-in. Rewriting it as compliance."

Theodora slammed her hand on the counter. "They erased their courage."

The echoes noticed us then. The customers turned, smiles too wide, eyes hollow. Their voices rose together, a sickly-sweet chant.

"Order brings peace. Order brings peace."

The fracture was here, vibrating in every word, every flicker of the sign.

Chris adjusted the tuner, sweat dripping down his temple. "I can isolate the real frequency—but I'll need an anchor!"

My eyes darted across the room. And then I saw it. On the wall, barely visible beneath layers of glitching paint, was a message scrawled in red:

THEY WANT OBEDIENCE. YOU NEED TRUTH. —A

"Over there!" I shouted, shoving past the frozen customers. My hand hit the graffiti, burning hot beneath my skin.

The room convulsed. The counter cracked. The voices warped into a deafening shriek.

For a heartbeat, I was inside both versions at once— one where the Four sat defiantly, sparking a movement, and one where they bowed their heads, submitting.

I pressed harder, fighting to hold the anchor.

And then Alex's voice whispered, sharp as glass: *"If they erase courage, they erase resistance. Don't let them."*

The sign above the counter shattered, fragments of neon raining down. The propaganda version collapsed, dissolving into static.

When the noise faded, only one version remained. The real one. Four young men, sitting tall, refusing to move.

Theodora's eyes shone with tears. "They're back. The truth is back."

But before relief could settle, Chris staggered. The tuner in his hands glowed with new text:

ECHO THREE: ACTIVE. WARNING: INSTABILITY RISING.

The ground shook beneath us.

This wasn't just about tracing echoes anymore.

The fractures were accelerating.

Chapter 13: Echo Three

The floor dissolved beneath us before we could catch our breath.

This time, the fall felt endless—static swallowing my senses, light stretching too thin to hold. When I landed, the air was thick, metallic, suffocating.

We were no longer in the past.

We were in the future.

A skyline loomed overhead, jagged towers of black steel. Drones swarmed like insects between them, beams of red light scanning the streets below. Digital billboards glowed against the smog-dark sky.

ORDER IS FREEDOM.

 TRUTH IS CHAOS.

 OBEDIENCE IS PEACE.

The words shifted every few seconds, cycling like mantras.

The streets were filled with people moving in perfect formation. Step for step. Breath for breath. Their faces expressionless, their eyes glowing faintly red. Not living—programmed.

Jalen's voice was tight. "This… this is us. If the fractures win."

Theodora gripped my arm so hard it hurt. "It's not just a warning. This is what they're building toward."

A siren wailed overhead. The drones shifted, beams locking onto us.

"Unregistered. Unregistered. Unregistered."

Chris's tuner squealed, the needle spiking so hard it nearly shattered the glass. "The signal's unstable. This Echo is collapsing."

The drone's dove.

We ran.

The ground shook beneath our feet as spotlights cut across the pavement. People in the crowd didn't react. They just kept marching, step after step, as though we didn't exist.

We ducked into an alley, hearts pounding. Theodora pressed her back against the wall, her face pale. "If this timeline locks in—if this becomes real—there won't be anything left to fight for."

Then I saw it.

Scrawled across the wall in red paint, glowing faintly against the steel:

THE FUTURE ISN'T FIXED. BURN THEIR BLUEPRINT. —A

My pulse quickened. Alex had been here too.

Chris raised the tuner, aligning it with the graffiti. The device wailed, frequencies colliding until the whole alley shook. The words pulsed brighter.

But before we could stabilize, one of the drones swooped down, its metallic limbs unfolding into jagged blades.

"Mila, hurry!" Jalen shouted, grabbing a pipe from the ground. He swung at the machine, sparks flying as metal clashed against metal.

The tuner screeched, then locked. The graffiti blazed, heat burning against my skin as I pressed my palm to it.

For a split second, the world split in two—one future of obedience, one blank and unformed.

Alex's voice whispered through the static, harsher than before: *"Don't just remember. Resist."*

The billboard above us shattered. The drones froze midair, glitching, collapsing into shards of light. The marching people flickered, then dissolved.

And then silence.

When I looked down, the tuner's screen displayed new text, but this time it pulsed with red, not green.

ECHO FOUR: ACTIVE. CRITICAL WARNING. FRACTURE CASCADE IMMINENT.

Chris's face went pale. "Cascade means…"
"Every fracture collapsing at once," Jalen finished.
Theodora's voice was barely a whisper. "If that happens, there won't be a timeline left."
And for the first time, I realized Alex's breadcrumbs weren't just about saving him.
They were about saving *everything*.

Chapter 14: Echo Four: The Cascade

We didn't jump this time.

We fell.

Light collapsed inward, crushing sound into silence, until my body felt like it was being pulled in every direction at once.

When the world reformed, it wasn't one place.

It was all of them.

We stood in a fractured city, its skyline torn apart and stitched back together like broken glass.

One block was Tulsa, glittering and alive.

The next—Tulsa burning, smoke choking the sky.

A diner blinked in and out of existence, one second filled with courage, the next poisoned with obedience.

Above us, the black steel towers of the future loomed, drones glitching as fireworks from a Fourth of July decades earlier bled across the sky.

Every timeline we'd touched was here, stacked and colliding.

Chris staggered, clutching his head. "This is the cascade. The fractures are converging!"

Jalen swore, pointing to the horizon. "Look!"

The world was unraveling. Whole streets folded in on themselves, collapsing into static. People froze mid-step, then split into duplicates—one smiling, one screaming, one fading into nothing.

Theodora's eyes brimmed with terror. "If this keeps spreading, reality itself will implode."

And then the whispers came. Not faint this time. Deafening.

"…fracture… remember… resist… obey…"

Voices layered, thousands of them, each pulling us in a different direction. My vision fractured—Tulsa, Greensboro, the future—all tugging at once.

"Mila!" Theodora grabbed my arm, grounding me. "Find the anchor!"

Chris's tuner spun violently, its needle slamming back and forth until sparks flew. He shouted over the roar.

"The signal's everywhere and nowhere—I can't isolate it!"

That's when I saw it.

In the center of the chaos stood a monument. Not a building. Not a machine. A mirror.

Its surface flickered with images—every choice, every fracture, every version of us we'd seen. And across its face, painted in glowing red strokes, were words that sent a chill through my bones:

**ONLY ONE TIMELINE SURVIVES. CHOOSE.
—A**

Jalen's voice broke. "He wants us to collapse the branches. Fuse them back into one."

Theodora shook her head violently. "No! If we choose wrong, we erase billions of lives—versions of us—forever."

Chris's face was pale, but his hands were steady as he lifted the tuner. "If we don't, there won't be any lives left to save."

The mirror pulsed, demanding.

I stepped closer. In its shifting surface, I saw myself—different versions of me.

One brave.

One broken.

One obedient.

One gone.

And behind them, Alex's face.

He looked straight at me, his voice cutting through the static like a blade.

"You've followed the echoes. Now decide. Do we restore the truth... or let them rewrite it forever?"

The ground shook violently, buildings collapsing into static.

Theodora shouted something I couldn't hear.
The drones screamed overhead.
The mirror burned brighter, waiting for my hand.
Waiting for my choice.

Chapter 15: The Choice

The mirror burned like a second sun, its surface a storm of faces—millions of versions of us, flickering in and out of existence.

One Mila was standing tall, defiant. Another was broken, shoulders hunched in surrender. Others were strangers—different hair, different scars, different lives—but all of them were me.

Behind them, Alex's reflection appeared. His face was sharp with urgency.

"Choose. Fuse the fractures. Restore one timeline before the cascade consumes everything."

Theodora's voice cracked. "Mila, don't—what if he's wrong? What if choosing erases the real one?"

Chris adjusted the tuner, sparks flying. "We don't have time! If the cascade completes, there won't be *any* timeline left!"

The ground heaved beneath us. Across the fractured city, entire blocks were collapsing into static. Echoes screamed as they dissolved—Tulsa's glittering towers falling into smoke, Greensboro's counter flickering out, drones from the future shattering like glass.

Jalen grabbed my shoulder. "Mila—listen to me. This isn't just about history. It's about control. If you fuse the timelines, you decide which version of the world survives."

The weight of it crushed me. Me. Not the Program. Not the machine. Me.

The mirror pulsed, and the voices rose:

"…remember… resist… obey… forget…"

I stepped closer, the heat blistering against my skin. Alex's eyes locked with mine through the storm of reflections.

"You've seen what obedience builds," he whispered. "You've seen what they erase. You've seen what they fear most—truth. If you want to save the world, don't give them the version they want. Give it the one that fights back."

Theodora screamed my name as the ground split apart. The mirror cracked. The choice had to be made—now. I raised my hand. And pressed it to the glass.

Chapter 16: Aftermath

When my palm touched the mirror, the world shattered.

Light exploded outward, a soundless detonation ripping through every fracture at once. For a heartbeat I was nowhere—then everywhere.

Tulsa alive. Tulsa burning. Greensboro defiant. Greensboro obedient. The future towers. The drones. All stacked like cards in a storm.

Then—silence.

I opened my eyes.

We were back at Site Zero.

The machine was dark. The coils no longer glowed.

The console, once alive with cascading text, displayed a single message:

TIMELINE STABILIZED.

Theodora gasped. "We did it."

Chris fell to his knees, the tuner clattering to the floor. "We actually did it."

But Jalen didn't look relieved. He stared at the darkened machine, his jaw tight. "No. Something's off. If the fractures really closed, why are we here? Why not back in our dorms? Why no debrief?"

I looked around. Site Zero seemed… different.
Cleaner. Too clean. The dust and condensation were
gone. The broken wires were neatly spliced. Even the
air smelled sterile.

And then the whisper came.

Not from the machine. From everywhere.

"…next stage…"

We froze.

The console flickered again. New text appeared:
**SIMULATION COMPLETE. INITIATING
PHASE TWO.**

My stomach turned. "What simulation?"

The walls around us shimmered. For a second, I
thought I saw another room behind them—white,
bright, clinical. Figures in lab coats moving. Screens
filled with data.

Then it was gone.

Theodora's hand found mine, fingers cold. "Mila…
what if none of it was real?"

Jalen swore under his breath. "Winters. He's been
testing us. All of this—Tulsa, Greensboro, the future—
just training modules."

Chris picked up the tuner. Its screen now displayed a
countdown:

00:05:00 – PHASE TWO ENTRY

"We're about to be moved," he whispered.

The ground beneath us vibrated. The machine pulsed once more, coils glowing faintly like a heartbeat.

I met Theodora's eyes. "If it's training…"

"…then phase two is the real thing," she finished.

And for the first time since I arrived, I felt something sharper than fear.

I felt ready.

Chapter 17: The Awakening

The countdown on Chris's tuner hit zero.

The machine's coils sparked, not with blue or red light this time, but a stark, blinding white. The chamber dissolved around us, walls peeling away like smoke.

And then we were standing in another room.

Bright. Sterile. Clinical.

The air smelled sharp, like antiseptic. The walls were smooth white panels, seamless, humming faintly as though alive. Transparent glass screens floated in midair, each displaying scrolling data: heart rates, brain waves, timelines overlayed with colored threads.

At the far end stood a line of figures in white coats, their faces hidden behind masks. Observing us. Measuring us.

Theodora stumbled back, her voice trembling. "No. No, this can't—"

Jalen's fists clenched. "They've been watching us the whole time."

A door hissed open, and Mr. Winters stepped inside. He wasn't wearing his usual pressed suit. This time, he wore the same white uniform as the others, his expression unreadable.

"Congratulations," he said smoothly, as though we had passed an exam. "You survived Phase One."

My voice shook. "Phase One? All of it—the fractures, Alex, Tulsa, Greensboro—none of it was real?"

"Real enough," Winters replied. "Every decision you made, every fear you faced, every sacrifice—it was all drawn from your memories, your histories, your world. We simulated it to measure your responses. To prepare you."

Chris's voice cracked. "Prepare us for what?"

Winters' eyes lingered on him before turning to the rest of us. "For the real thing. Time travel is not a fantasy, nor is it forgiving. If you enter untrained, you'll fracture reality beyond repair. But if you can survive the echoes—even in simulation—you may have a chance in the field."

Theodora stepped forward, her voice sharp. "And Alex? Was he just part of the test too?"

For the first time, Winters hesitated. A flicker in his expression, gone almost as quickly as it appeared.

"Alex was a variable," he said at last. "A previous recruit who did not adapt to training. His breadcrumbs were intentional. We left them for you."

The words stung like a blade. Alex—real, but repurposed. A warning disguised as a ghost.

I swallowed hard. "So, what happens now?"

Winters gestured to the glowing doorway behind him. "Now you rest. Tomorrow, Phase Two begins. You've proven you can survive simulated fractures. Next, you'll survive the real ones."

The glass screens flickered again, briefly showing images, I didn't recognize—places blurred by static, events unfolding across different years. I saw fire, oceans swallowing cities, faces I didn't know calling out in silence.

And beneath them all, a single phrase repeated, stamped across the data:

INITIATING FIELD TRAINING.

The door hissed wider. Winters' gaze pinned me. "Step through. The future is waiting."

My chest tightened, but my legs carried me forward. Because whatever the truth was, whatever they were preparing us for—this was only the beginning.

Chapter 18: The Facility

The doorway swallowed us in white light, and when it faded, we were somewhere new.

Rows of glass corridors stretched in every direction, their walls glowing faintly with streams of data. Through them, I caught glimpses of other recruits— some walking in tight formations, others hooked to machines, their eyes flickering rapidly beneath closed lids.

"This place is massive," Chris whispered. His voice echoed too loudly in the sterile air.

Jalen's jaw tightened. "It's a hive."

Winters led us down a hall until we reached a chamber of transparent walls. Inside, a group of recruits ran through combat drills against projections that moved faster than anything human. Across another corridor, I saw two recruits strapped into chairs, their minds linked to a swirling field of light—echo simulations like the ones we'd survived, only harsher, sharper. One of them screamed. The instructors didn't react.

"This is the Nexus," Winters said flatly. "Our central training hub. What you endured before was child's play. Phase Two tests the body as much as the mind.

You will learn to resist disorientation, to anchor without external aids, and to endure temporal bleed."

Theodora frowned. "Temporal bleed?"

"You'll find out soon enough," Winters replied. His calm made it worse than if he'd shouted.

He stopped before a sealed door, pressed his hand to the panel, and the glass slid open. Inside were four cots, a table, and walls lined with thin bands of light—our quarters.

"This will be your living space until further notice. You train. You study. You rest. Nothing more." He turned to leave but paused in the doorway. "One last thing. From this point forward, failure has consequences. This is not simulation anymore. The risks are real."

And then he was gone.

Silence settled over us.

Theodora sat heavily on one of the cots, staring at the floor. "So, everything we just fought through… none of it was real."

Jalen shook his head. "Doesn't matter. The fear was real. The choices were real. That's what they wanted."

Chris fiddled with the tuner, though it was now dark, unresponsive. "If this is the real world... what if the fractures are real too?"

His words sank into me like stones. Because even here, in this sterile cage, I swore I heard it again—faint static, whispering at the edge of my thoughts.

Remember.

Chapter 19: The First Trial

We hadn't been in our quarters for more than a few hours when the alarms sounded.

The walls lit up in crimson bands, and a metallic voice filled the room.

"Recruits 17-A through 17-D: Report to Chamber Six. Trial commencing."

Theodora shot me a look. "That's us."

We followed the glowing corridor until it opened into a vast circular arena. Its walls were seamless white; its ceiling lost in shadows. Rows of masked observers stood behind glass above us, silent, recording every move.

Winters waited in the center, hands clasped behind his back.

"Phase Two begins now," he said. "Your first trial: stabilization under stress."

The floor shifted beneath us, panels rearranging into jagged terrain—broken stone, twisted steel, flickering streetlamps. For a moment, it felt like we'd been dropped into the ruins of a city.

Then the static began.

At first it was faint, a whisper. Then it roared, tearing through the air until the walls flickered like a dying signal. Figures emerged from the distortion—echoes, their faces blank, their bodies glitching as though pulled from fractured timelines.

Theodora gasped. "They're sending us back in?"

"No," Jalen muttered, fists clenched. "They're bringing it *here*."

Winters' voice cut through the chaos. "Anchor the timeline. Or be consumed by it."

The echoes lunged.

Chris scrambled with the tuner, but it stayed dead in his hands. "It's not working! They disabled it!"

"Then we stabilize ourselves," I shouted.

The first echo hit Jalen, knocking him to the ground. Its body rippled like liquid, its face flickering between strangers. He kicked it off, but another was already closing in.

I felt the static searing into my skull, tearing at my memories. For a moment I was back in Tulsa, then in Greensboro, then staring at the future's black towers. My mind buckled under the weight of too many realities.

Anchor yourself, I told myself. *Anchor or drown.*

I dropped to my knees, pressing my palms to the fractured ground. I pictured one truth: the marble steps at the rally where it all began. The sunlight. The crowd's voices. The invitation. I clung to it with everything I had.

The static wavered. The arena flickered.

"Focus!" I screamed at the others. "Pick a memory! Something that's yours, not theirs!"

Theodora squeezed her eyes shut, whispering about her grandmother's voice singing her to sleep. Chris muttered numbers, equations, grounding himself in logic. Jalen shouted the name of his little brother.

One by one, the echoes staggered, their forms collapsing into static.

The arena brightened. The ground stabilized.

And then, silence.

The echoes were gone. The trial was over.

Above us, the observers scribbled notes, their faces hidden. Winters stepped forward, his expression unreadable.

"Not elegant," he said coldly. "But effective. You anchored. That is the first step toward survival."

He let the silence linger before adding: "Next time, there will be no warning. No safe chamber. Remember that."

He turned, leaving us in the wreckage of the trial.

My body trembled, every nerve on fire. But beneath the fear, something else pulsed—something sharper. For the first time, I knew we weren't just surviving training.
We were learning how to fight.

Chapter 20: The Second Trial

We were given no time to recover.

Hours—maybe minutes—after the first trial, the alarms returned.

"Recruits 17-A through 17-D: Report to Chamber Eleven. Trial commencing."

Theodora groaned, exhausted, but there was no choice. The corridors glowed red, guiding us forward until the glass parted again.

This chamber was different. Smaller. Colder. A ring of mirrors lined the walls, each surface shimmering faintly as though it hid something behind it.

Winters' voice echoed from overhead this time, disembodied.

"Trial Two: Distortion. You will confront fractured reflections of yourselves. Anchor against your own collapse."

The mirrors rippled.

And then *we* stepped out.

Copies—each of us duplicated, their features sharp, their eyes glowing faintly with static. My double tilted her head, a cruel smile tugging her mouth.

"You think you're the original?" she asked, her voice my voice, twisted. "You're just one of a thousand

Milas, all screaming you're the real one. Which one do you think survives?"

My stomach churned.

Theodora's reflection sneered. "You've always been afraid. Always clinging to someone else's fight."

Chris's double laughed, holding a tuner that *worked.* "You'll never match me. You'll always be a step behind."

Jalen's reflection stepped closer, his eyes cold. "You let your brother down. Again. And again. And again."

The chamber spun. I couldn't tell if their words were lies or truths, I'd buried too deep.

Theodora staggered back, clutching her head. "They're inside our thoughts—"

"Don't listen!" Jalen shouted, but even his voice sounded fractured, echoing in my skull.

My reflection lunged. I stumbled, grappling with her, but she was stronger, faster. Her hands closed around my throat.

Anchor yourself, I thought desperately. *Find the truth.* But what if she was right? What if I wasn't the original? What if I was just another simulation?

Theodora screamed. Chris shouted my name.

And then, through the chaos, a whisper cut through:

Remember what they erased.

Alex's voice.

It sliced the doubt like a blade. I shoved my reflection back, my palm pressing against her chest. "You're not me. You're a shadow. I choose who I am."

She convulsed, her form splintering into static before collapsing.

Around me, the others fought back. Theodora tore through her reflection, grounding herself in her grandmother's song. Chris shouted equations like a mantra until his double shattered. Jalen, trembling but defiant, roared his brother's name as he crushed his reflection into fragments.

And then, silence.

The mirrors cracked and dissolved, leaving only us. Winters' voice returned, flat and calm. "You survived. Barely. Remember this lesson: your greatest enemy in the fractures is not the past, nor the future. It is yourselves."

The chamber went dark. The floor shifted beneath us, carrying us back to the corridor.

Theodora's voice was raw. "If that wasn't real…, why does it hurt like it was?"

Jalen's hands were shaking. "Because maybe it was. Maybe we're still in their game."

I glanced at the walls, at the glowing data that never stopped pulsing, and for the first time I wondered if we would ever know when the simulation truly ended.

Chapter 21: Cracks in the Program

The corridor carried us back to our quarters. The door sealed behind us with a soft hiss, locking us inside.

No one spoke for a long time.

Theodora finally broke the silence. "That wasn't training. That was torture."

Chris sat hunched over the dark tuner, still trying to coax life from it. "If it was real," he muttered.

Jalen shot him a sharp look. "It *was* real. We bled. We felt it."

Chris didn't look up. "So did we in the first simulations. What's the difference? How do we know this isn't just another layer?"

Theodora rubbed her temples. "Don't start that again—"

"No," I cut in. "He's right."

They all turned toward me.

"Think about it," I said. "Every trial has been built from *us*—our memories, our fears, our pasts. Winters said it was Phase Two, but what if this is just another test? A deeper simulation to see how far we'll break?"

Theodora shook her head. "But Winters is here. The instructors. The recruits in the other chambers. We saw them."

"Did we?" Jalen countered. "Or did they show us what they wanted us to see?"

The words hung heavy in the air.

Chris finally sighed and set the tuner down. "There's one way to know. Alex."

At his name, my heart clenched.

He leaned forward. "If Alex was a failed recruit like Winters said, then why do we keep hearing his voice? Why do his breadcrumbs show up in every fracture—even here? Either Winters is lying, or Alex found a way to push through the system."

Theodora whispered, "So he's alive?"

"Or what's left of him is," Jalen muttered darkly.

I couldn't let the thought go. *Remember what they erased. Don't just remember—resist.* His words weren't random. They were deliberate.

I lowered my voice. "Then we find him. If Winters won't give us the truth, we dig for it ourselves."

Chris perked up, eyes gleaming with quiet rebellion. "The systems here are locked, but not impenetrable. If I can get the tuner online again, I might be able to access their data streams."

Jalen frowned. "If they catch you—"

"They'll do worse than fail me," Chris finished. "I know."

Theodora crossed her arms. "Then we help. No more walking into their trials blind."

For the first time, a spark lit in my chest. Fear hadn't gone anywhere—it was still coiled tight in me—but it wasn't the only thing.

There was defiance too.

"Alright," I said. "From here on, we play their game on the surface. But beneath it—we follow Alex's trail. Whatever he wanted us to see, we find it."

Silence followed, but no one disagreed.

Somewhere beyond the walls, alarms echoed faintly. Another group's trial. Another test. Another lie.

And I swore I heard it again, hidden beneath the hum of the Nexus itself.

Resist.

Chapter 22: The Breach

The next morning, Winters' voice summoned us again. **"Recruits 17-A through 17-D: Report to Chamber Nine."**

We followed in silence, our plan unspoken but heavy between us. Chris carried the tuner tucked against his chest, its cracked screen dark. He'd been working on it all night, soldering circuits with scraps from the quarters, rerouting its power cell.

As we entered Chamber Nine, Winters was already waiting. The floor reconfigured into a barren desert, the horizon endless and shimmering with heat. Above us, observers filled the glass gallery, silent as ever.

"Trial Three," Winters announced. "Sustainment. No anchors. No assistance. You will endure the fracture until it stabilizes. Or you will not."

The static came fast this time, rolling across the sand like a storm. Figures emerged from it—echoes again, but twisted, skeletal, their bodies crackling with fractured light.

I braced myself, but Chris didn't move toward them. Instead, he crouched low, the tuner already in his hands.

Jalen hissed, "Not now—"

"Now or never," Chris muttered.

He flicked the switch. For a second, nothing. Then the tuner whined, its cracked screen lighting faintly with static. He twisted the dial, forcing it higher. The static in the chamber responded, rippling like a disturbed pool of water.

The echoes froze.

Winters' voice boomed overhead. "What are you doing, recruit?"

Chris ignored him, hands steady despite the sweat running down his face. The tuner screeched, then cleared into a single frequency. Words formed across the broken screen, jagged but unmistakable:

REMEMBER. —A

Theodora gasped. "It's him."

Winters barked an order from above, but the glass between us shimmered, his voice cutting into static. The entire chamber flickered.

Chris twisted the dial again. The tuner wailed—and then Alex's voice filled the room.

Not an echo. Not a hallucination. His real voice, strained but sharp:

"If you can hear this, you've pierced their veil. Good. That means you're close. Don't trust the trials. Don't

trust Winters. They're not training you—they're rewriting you. They want you to forget who you were, so you'll obey who they want you to be."

The chamber shook violently. The skeletal echoes disintegrated into shards of light, collapsing into the sand.

The observers above pounded on the glass, shouting to each other, but their words didn't reach us.

Winters' voices finally cut through, low and deadly calm. "Enough."

The chamber blinked—and the desert was gone. We were back in our quarters, the cots perfectly aligned, the bands of light humming.

The tuner in Chris's hands went dark again, its cracked screen smoking.

No one moved. No one spoke.

Then Theodora whispered, "He's alive."

Jalen's eyes burned. "And he's inside their system."

I clenched my fists, my pulse hammering. Alex wasn't just a breadcrumb anymore. He was fighting with us.

And if Winters thought we were going to keep playing his game, he was wrong.

Chapter 23: Sparks of Rebellion

We expected punishment.

Instead, the next day passed in silence. No summons. No alarms. Just the four of us locked in our quarters, the sterile hum of the Nexus filling the space.

It was worse than a trial. At least in the trials, we knew where to direct the fear. Here, it just festered.

Chris paced endlessly, muttering equations under his breath. Theodora lay on her cot staring at the ceiling, her lips moving soundlessly, repeating her grandmother's lullaby. Jalen sat against the wall, fists clenched, jaw tight.

Finally, I couldn't take it anymore.

"They're waiting for us to break," I said.

Jalen looked up. "Then let's give them something else."

Chris stopped pacing. "You mean—?"

"Alex," I said. "He cut through once. If he can reach us from inside, maybe we can reach him too."

Chris's eyes lit with a dangerous spark. "I thought about that. The tuner's fried, but this whole place runs on layered signals. If I can piggyback on one—"

Theodora sat up sharply. "Chris, if they catch you—"

"They already know," he snapped. "Winters heard Alex's message. The only reason we're still breathing is because he wants to see what we'll do next."

Silence stretched, broken only by the hum of the walls.

Jalen stood. "Then let's stop giving him obedience."

I felt something stir in my chest—fear, yes, but also fire. "We don't wait for the next trial. We start one ourselves."

Theodora's eyes darted between us. "You're talking about open rebellion inside the Program."

"Yes," I said simply. "We stop being their recruits and start being their problem."

Chris was already moving; prying open the wall panel above his cot with a stolen fragment of steel. Wires sparked beneath his fingers. "If I can trigger a feedback surge, I might be able to punch a hole in their firewall. Long enough to see what's buried in their system."

Jalen moved to the door, pressing his ear against the seam. "I'll keep watch. If Winters comes—"

"He'll come," I said. "But let him. At least this time it'll be on our terms."

Theodora's hands shook as she stood to join Chris at the panel. "If this gets us killed, I'll haunt you."

"Deal," Chris muttered, sparks flying.

And then, for the first time since we'd arrived, the sterile white walls flickered. A ripple spread across the room, and in the distortion, words appeared across the band of light above the cots.

RESIST. —A

Theodora gasped. "He's here."

Chris grinned through sweat. "No. He's with us."

Alarms blared. The corridor outside lit up in blood-red pulses.

"Security breach. Quarantine imminent."

I turned to the others, heart pounding, but my voice steady.

"This is it. We've been waiting for our chance. Now we make it."

The door hissed. Shadows moved on the other side.

We weren't recruits anymore.

We were rebels.

Chapter 24: Quarantined

The door slid open with a hiss, and for a moment, we thought we were ready.

We weren't.

Figures in white armor surged into the quarters, faceless behind mirrored visors. They moved with mechanical precision, faster than we could react. Jalen lunged first, swinging the shard of steel Chris had used on the panel, but one of the guards caught his arm mid-swing, twisted, and dropped him with a single strike. Theodora screamed and tried to run, but two more blocked the door, shoving her hard against the wall. Chris clutched the tuner like a weapon, sparks still stuttering from its cracked edges. "Don't touch her!"

The guard nearest him raised a baton crackling with blue current. Chris didn't get the chance to finish his threat. The baton connected, and his body spasmed before crumpling to the ground.

I barely had time to shout his name before a hand like iron clamped around my arm. I twisted, kicked, fought, but the grip didn't loosen. Another guard forced me to my knees; my face pressed against the sterile floor. Above the chaos, Winters' voice cut through, calm and sharp as a blade.

"Enough."

The guards froze immediately.

Winters stepped into the quarters, his uniform immaculate, his expression unreadable. He glanced at the sparking panel, the unconscious Chris, the rest of us restrained.

"I warned you," he said simply.

He paced slowly, his voice never rising. "You confuse survival with rebellion. You think because you saw one message, one crack in the system, that you've uncovered the truth. But let me remind you: you're still here. You're still *inside*. Every move you make, every breath you take, I allow."

Theodora spat blood, her voice trembling with rage. "Alex warned us—he told us not to trust you!"

For the first time, Winters' mask slipped. His eyes narrowed.

"Alex," he said softly. "Still haunting you. That failed recruit was meant to be erased. He left nothing but corrupted data, broken code clinging to your simulations. If you think you can follow his trail, you'll only end where he did—destroyed."

My heart pounded. "Then why does he keep finding us? Why does he keep slipping through?"

Winters stopped, his gaze piercing into me. For a moment, something flickered there—frustration, maybe fear. Then it was gone.

He turned to the guards. "Quarantine them. No trials. No quarters. Isolation."

The guards hauled us to our feet, dragging us down the corridor as alarms still echoed. Behind us, the panel Chris had ripped open sealed itself seamlessly, the words **RESIST. —A** vanishing into sterile white.

As they forced us into separate cells, cold and empty, one thought burned in my chest:

We had failed.

But Alex hadn't.

Not yet.

They dragged me into a cell no bigger than a closet. The walls were smooth white, seamless, humming faintly like the corridors. No cot. No light but the faint glow from above. No door once it sealed shut — just emptiness.

At first, I screamed. My fists pounded the walls, my throat raw, but the walls didn't yield. The sound bounced back at me, mocking.

Time dissolved.

Maybe hours passed. Maybe days. There was no clock, no cycle, nothing to mark the difference between waking and dreaming. My body ached from the cold floor. My stomach burned from hunger. My mouth was dry as dust.

That's when the whispers began.

"...you're not real... you're one of many... choose obedience and the pain stops..."

The voices were my own. My reflection from the second trial. Winters' calm tone. My mother's voice, warped into something cruel.

"You don't matter. You're replaceable. You're already erased."

I pressed my hands to my ears, but the voices crawled through my skull, worming deep. The walls shimmered. Faces appeared, fractured versions of me, all sneering.

You're a shadow.

You're a failure.

You'll never anchor again.

I curled tighter on the floor, my breath shallow, my chest trembling. Maybe Winters was right. Maybe we'd never left the simulations. Maybe Alex was nothing but corrupted code. Maybe I was already gone.

Then—

"Mila."

Not a whisper. Not a hallucination. His voice.

I sat up sharply. "Alex?"

The walls flickered, and for the briefest second, I saw him — not fractured, not static. Him. Standing in a corridor that wasn't mine, eyes fierce, jaw tight.

"You're stronger than this," he said. His voice shook with urgency. "Don't let them take you apart."

Tears blurred my vision. "I don't know what's real anymore—"

"That's the point," Alex cut in. "They want to strip you down until obedience feels like the only truth. Don't give it to them. Anchor to yourself. Anchor to me if you have to. But don't break."

The walls trembled. Alarms wailed faintly outside, muffled. The vision stuttered, static eating at his outline.

"Alex!" I reached for him, my hand colliding with smooth white wall.

His form flickered. "They can't hold me out forever. I'm in the cracks. Keep resisting. The fractures you saw—Tulsa, Greensboro, the future—none of that was wasted. It was all preparing you."

The static surged. His voice warped.

"…next stage… field test… real fractures coming…"

Then he was gone.

The walls returned to sterile white. My cell was silent again.

But I wasn't.

I pressed my palm flat against the wall where he'd appeared, my voice low but steady.

"I'll resist. I'll remember. I'll fight."

And for the first time since the cell closed, the whispers didn't answer back.

Chapter 25: Reunion

The door dissolved without warning.

For a second, I thought it was another hallucination, another trick of the white walls. But the opening didn't fade. A guard in mirrored armor stood waiting, silent, gesturing for me to step out.

I forced my shaking legs to move. The corridor outside hummed with its endless sterile glow. I kept my head high, even though every nerve screamed to collapse. They led me back to our quarters. The door sealed shut behind me, and suddenly I wasn't alone.

Theodora was curled on her cot, eyes hollow, lips moving faintly as if still whispering her lullaby. Jalen sat against the wall, fists clenched tight enough to draw blood, his eyes red and wild. Chris lay flat on his back, the broken tuner resting on his chest like a shield.

Theodora looked up first. Her eyes widened. "Mila... you're here." Her voice cracked, hoarse from silence.

"I'm here," I said.

Jalen pushed himself up, his voice sharp. "How long were you under?"

"I don't know." I glanced between them. "How long for you?"

They exchanged looks. None of us had answers.

Chris finally spoke, his voice flat. "Long enough."
Theodora's hands trembled as she reached for me.
"They whispered to me. My grandmother's voice, but
wrong. Kept telling me to forget. To let go." Her voice
dropped. "I almost did."
Jalen's jaw tightened. "They showed me my brother.
Over and over. Each time, I failed him again. Each
time, he disappeared sooner."
Chris turned his head toward the wall. "They didn't
show me anything. Just silence. Like I wasn't even
worth breaking."
The words cut deep.
I sat down, forcing strength into my voice. "They tried
to break me too. But they can't erase us. Not all of us."
Theodora shook her head. "You don't understand—"
"I do." My voice sharpened. "Because Alex was
there."
They all froze.
Jalen's eyes narrowed. "You saw him?"
"He spoke to me," I said. "Clearer than ever before.
He's inside their cracks, fighting them. He said
everything we went through—the echoes, the
fractures—it was all preparing us. For something real.
Something coming."

Chris pushed himself upright, clutching the dead tuner. His face lit with a flicker of life. "Then he's not gone."

"No," I said firmly. "And neither are we. They want us broken, obedient. But Alex is proof we can resist."

Silence hung heavy, but it was different this time. Not despair. Not defeat.

A spark.

Jalen finally nodded, slow and grim. "Then we don't stop. Not until we know what's really waiting outside their walls."

Theodora's voice shook, but she whispered, "Resist."

Chris echoed it softly. "Resist."

I clenched my fists, holding onto the word like an anchor. "Together."

For the first time since quarantine, it felt like the walls were listening.

Chapter 26: The Invisible Trial

The next morning, no alarms sounded. No summons. No Winters.

Just silence.

We stayed in our quarters, waiting, restless. Hours passed—or what felt like hours. The white bands of light on the walls never dimmed.

Chris tapped the dead tuner against his palm, muttering, "They've cut us off. No trials, no data, nothing."

Theodora shifted uneasily. "Maybe it's over?"

"No," Jalen said flatly. "This is the trial."

He was right.

The walls hummed faintly, louder than usual. Almost like breathing.

Then the changes began.

At first, they were small. The cot beneath me was suddenly gone when I turned to sit. Theodora's hair, for a flicker of a second, was short instead of long. Chris muttered an equation on repeat, and when he stopped, I realized he'd already said it a dozen times, the moment looping.

We were still in quarantine. Still in our quarters. But something was off.

"They're testing us," I whispered. "Reality's shifting."

Theodora stood, panic rising in her voice. "I don't— I don't know what's real anymore—"

The wall behind her rippled. For an instant, it showed another room: her grandmother's house, warm light spilling through the window. Theodora gasped, stepping toward it—

Jalen grabbed her arm. "No! It's bait!"

The room snapped back to sterile white.

Then it was my turn.

The wall shimmered again, this time showing the marble steps of the rally. Alex stood there, smiling like he had that first day. His voice carried across the impossible distance.

"Leave breadcrumbs, Mila. You've always known how to find me."

I felt myself leaning forward, hand outstretched—

Chris shouted, "It's another construct! Fight it!"

I blinked. Alex was gone. Just the wall again.

The air grew colder. Our breaths fogged. Words formed on the band of light above us, glowing red:

TRIAL IN PROGRESS. DO NOT ALERT SUBJECTS.

My blood ran cold. "We weren't supposed to see that."

Chris's grin was bitter. "Then maybe we're not the ones failing."

The walls shimmered again, faster now. Flashes of different places, different times—Tulsa, Greensboro, the future towers, all colliding in quick bursts. My head spun with the overload.

Theodora dropped to her knees, sobbing. "I can't— I can't anchor—"

Jalen crouched beside her, gripping her shoulders. "Anchor to us. Not to them. To *us*."

I pressed my hand to the wall, forcing my voice steady. "They want us fractured. They want us obedient. But if we hold to each other—just each other—they can't erase us."

Chris raised the dead tuner like a totem. "Then let's give them nothing but static."

We closed ranks, backs pressed together, eyes shut tight against the illusions. The walls pulsed, the whispers rose, but we held.

And then—silence.

The room stilled. The walls smoothed. The red words faded.

The band of light above flickered one last time, and for a heartbeat, I swore I saw Alex's message carved into it, faint but there:

GOOD. YOU'RE LEARNING. —A

When the room settled again, we were shaking, exhausted—but still together.

For the first time, I realized something terrifying.

We hadn't beaten the Program.

But we were starting to *see through it.*

Chapter 27: The Bleed

It started with a sound. A low, rattling hum, deeper than the usual sterile buzz of the walls. It vibrated through the floor, through our bones.

Chris sat bolt upright on his cot. "That's not the normal hum."

Theodora frowned. "What is it?"

"The system," he said. "Failing."

The band of light above our heads flickered wildly. For a second, the sterile white walls were gone — replaced by the fractured skyline of the future towers, drones screaming overhead. Then it was gone again. Then back.

The room shifted around us in bursts of impossible geography: Tulsa's glittering streets. Greensboro's lunch counter. The white facility. Over and over, faster, and faster.

"It's bleeding," Chris whispered. "The fractures are leaking in."

Theodora clutched her head, her voice trembling. "I thought this was the real world—"

Jalen grabbed her shoulders, steadying her. "That's the point. It's not. Not fully. And now it's coming apart."

I pressed my palm to the flickering wall. Heat burned against my skin, the static so strong it buzzed up my arm. Through the shifting images, I swore I saw Winters — not in control, but shouting at masked technicians, his face pale.

"They can't stop it," I murmured. "We're seeing what's behind their curtain."

Chris scrambled to the broken tuner, prying at its casing. "If Alex is in the cracks, this might be our chance to talk to him directly."

The floor tilted beneath us, throwing us all off balance. The walls tore open like paper, revealing nothing but static beyond. Through it, echoes moved — not projections this time, but shapes dragging themselves through the bleed, glitching, collapsing, reforming.

One of them reached out, its face flickering between all of ours.

"You're not ready," it whispered in a thousand voices at once. "But you will be."

Theodora screamed. Jalen pulled her back, but the echo didn't attack — it just reached, as if offering a hand.

Chris shouted over the rising hum. "It's not attacking! It's trying to merge!"

The static surged higher, the bleed swallowing the walls, the floor, the ceiling.

I grabbed the tuner from Chris's hands, twisting the dial until sparks burned my fingers. "Alex," I shouted into the noise. "If you're here—help us anchor!"

For a heartbeat, everything froze.

Then a voice cut through, sharp and clear, echoing from nowhere and everywhere:

"Field test imminent. Survive the breach. This is your last simulation."

The walls exploded outward in light.

And we were falling again.

Chapter 28: The Breach

We hit the ground hard.

Not the sterile floor of the facility. Not Tulsa. Not Greensboro. Not the towers of the future.

All of them.

The world around us twisted, fractured, every timeline we had seen colliding at once. Skyscrapers from the future split through the streets of Tulsa, burning against the sky. The Greensboro counter flickered in and out of existence, sometimes whole, sometimes shattered. Fireworks exploded above the static-streaked horizon, dissolving into screaming drones.

We were in the middle of the cascade again — but raw, violent, uncontrolled.

Chris scrambled to his feet, clutching the dead tuner.

"It's the bleed. They dumped us inside the breach itself!"

Theodora screamed as an echo lurched from the static — not faceless this time, but *me*. My reflection, snarling, eyes glowing red. Another echo followed, this one Jalen, its mouth twisted into a scream.

"They're pulling from us," Jalen shouted. "Every memory, every fear!"

The echoes lunged.

I dodged, swinging a broken length of steel torn from the fractured ground. My double caught it bare-handed, sparks flying as metal hit static flesh. She shoved me back, stronger, faster, relentless.

"Anchor!" I screamed. "Find your memory!"

Theodora clutched her head, whispering her grandmother's song through choked sobs. Her echo shrieked, then collapsed into static.

Jalen roared his brother's name, driving a shard of rubble straight through his double's chest. It dissolved in light.

Chris staggered, his reflection towering over him, holding a perfect, functional tuner. "You'll never win," it hissed.

Chris grit his teeth, raising the broken device in his hands. "I don't need a perfect tuner. I just need *this one*." He smashed it against his double's chest. Sparks erupted, static screamed, and both the reflection and tuner vanished in a burst of light.

The ground convulsed beneath us, tearing open into a chasm of raw static. The sky flickered between futures—cities burning, oceans rising, towers collapsing. My lungs burned, my body heavy, but I forced myself up, gripping the steel tighter.

"Hold together!" I shouted. "Anchor to each other, not to them!"

We formed a circle, backs pressed together, echoes swarming from the static. Hundreds of them—versions of us, of Winters, of strangers—faces we knew and didn't. All screaming, all rushing closer.

The static roared.

And then, through the chaos, Alex's voice thundered above it all:

"This is the last wall. Survive this breach and you'll see the truth."

The echoes shrieked and dove. We braced ourselves, every nerve on fire, every anchor burning in our chests. And then the world exploded in light.

Chapter 29: The Truth

Light swallowed everything.

I braced for the impact, for the echoes, for the static to tear us apart. But when my eyes opened—

I was lying on a table.

Not in the breach. Not in the facility. Somewhere else. Bright white lights glared down. Cold metal pressed against my back. My arms and legs were strapped, sensors running up my skin. A steady beeping filled the air.

I gasped, fighting against the restraints.

"Mila."

I turned my head. Theodora was on a table beside mine, blinking awake, strapped the same way. Chris lay to my left, monitors wired into his chest, his eyes flickering rapidly as though dreaming. Jalen groaned on another table, struggling against his bonds.

We were all there. All alive.

And above us—observers. Not behind glass this time but standing over us in the flesh. White coats. Masks. Machines humming softly behind them.

One of them leaned closer, scribbling notes. His voice was calm, clinical.

"Subject group seventeen. Simulation complete."

My heart froze.

Another figure adjusted a dial, watching Chris's monitor spike. "Cognitive anchors intact. Memory recall tested. Emotional fracture within acceptable limits."

A third nodded. "They're ready for field deployment." The words sank into me like a blade. *Simulation complete.*

It was all still inside. Every fracture. Every trial. Every rebellion.

Not real.

A hiss filled the room as the restraints released. I sat up sharply, heart pounding, head spinning.

Winters stood in the corner. No mask this time. His expression was unreadable, but his eyes gleamed with something I hadn't seen before—satisfaction.

"Congratulations," he said smoothly. "You've passed."

Theodora's voice cracked. "Passed... what?"

Winters' smile was thin. "Phase One. Preparation. You've proven capable of surviving simulated fractures. Now... the real ones await."

Behind him, a door slid open. Beyond it was no sterile corridor, no white chamber.

It was a launch bay. Massive, metal, alive with humming machinery. At its center stood a towering construct of copper and steel — the same coils as the machine in Site Zero, only whole. Active.

The hum vibrated in my chest.

Jalen whispered, "This... this is real."

Winters gestured toward the machine. "Welcome to your future. Phase Two begins now."

My pulse thundered as I stepped off the table, the others beside me, the truth pressing down like gravity.

We hadn't been fighting the past.

We'd been training for the future.

www.ingramcontent.com/pod-product-compliance
Lightning Source LLC
Chambersburg PA
CBHW050832180626
46814CB00004B/1583